Chapter I
Vincennes School Corporation

Lily Takes A Walk

Unicorn is a registered trademark of E. P. Dutton.
Library of Congress number 87-8894
ISBN 0-525-44699-0

Published in the United States by
Dutton Children's Books,
a division of Penguin Books USA Inc.

Originally published in England by Blackie and Son Ltd,
7 Leicester Place, London WC2H 7BP

Printed in Hong Kong by South China Printing Co.
First Unicorn Edition 1991
10 9 8 7 6 5 4 3 2 1

Lily Takes A Walk
Satoshi Kitamura

DUTTON CHILDREN'S BOOKS
NEW YORK

Lily likes going for walks
with her dog, Nicky.

Sometimes they walk for hours and hours
until the sun starts to slip down
behind the hill.

Even when it begins to get dark,
Lily is never scared, because
Nicky is there with her.

Today on the way home,
she does the shopping
for her mother.

Then she stops for a moment
to look at the evening star.
"Look, Nicky," she says.
"That's called the Dog Star."

As Lily walks past Mrs. Hall's window, she waves.

Bats flitter and swoop in the evening sky.
"Aren't they clever, Nicky?" says Lily.
"Not far now."

She stops by the bridge to say good night
to the gulls and the ducks on the canal.

At last she comes to her own corner.
This is the best moment of all.
She can see the light in her window
and smell her supper cooking.

Lily's mother and father always like to hear
what she has seen on her walks.

Before long, it is time for bed.
Nicky is already in his basket.
"We had a good walk today,
didn't we?" says Lily.
"Good night, Nicky.
Sleep tight."